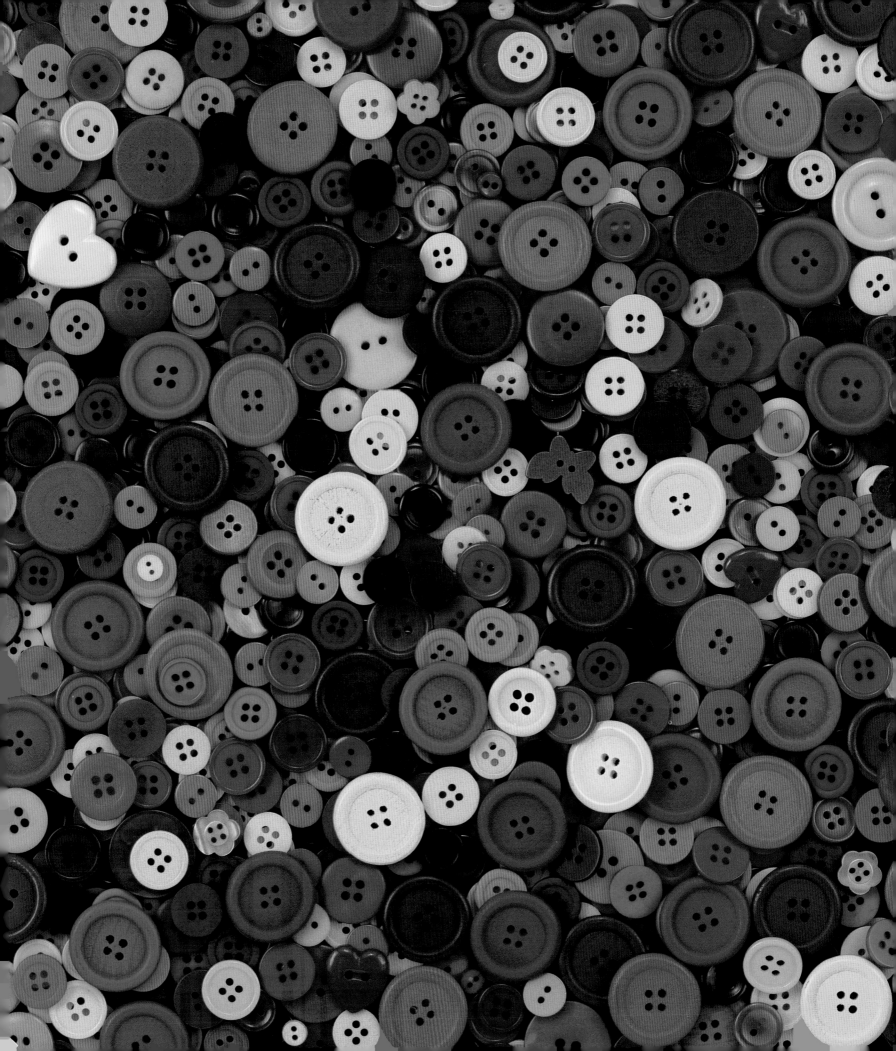

1, 2, Buckle My Shoe

Anna Grossnickle Hines

Harcourt, Inc.

Orlando   Austin   New York   San Diego   London

Manufactured in China

Shut
the door.

Pick up
sticks.

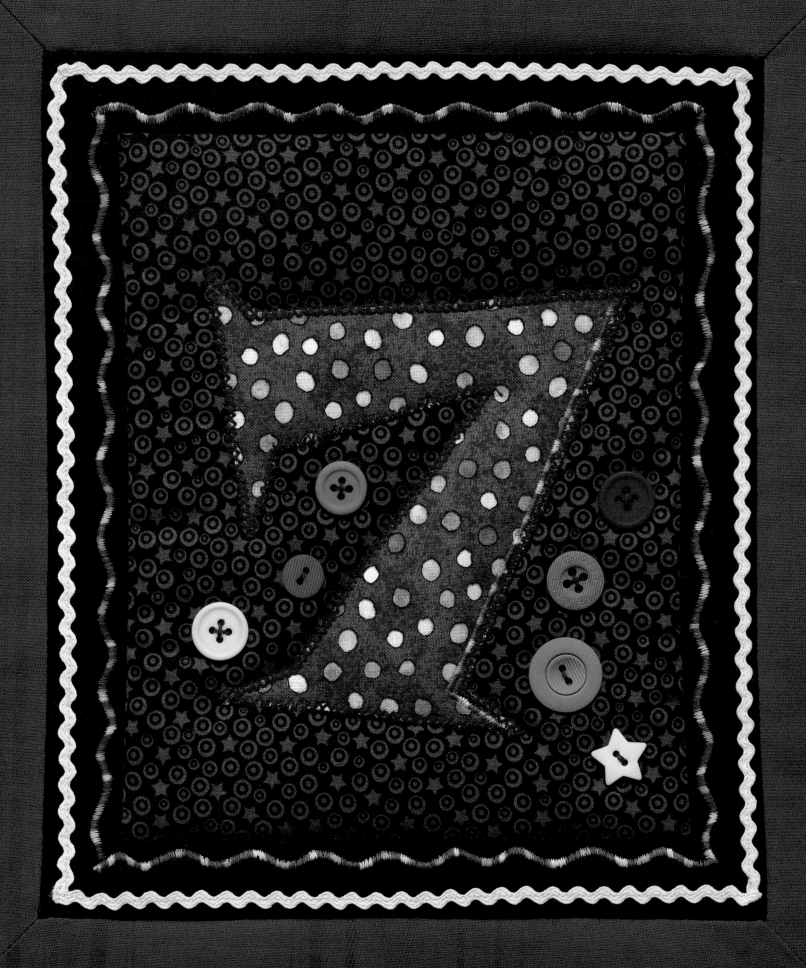

Open the gate.

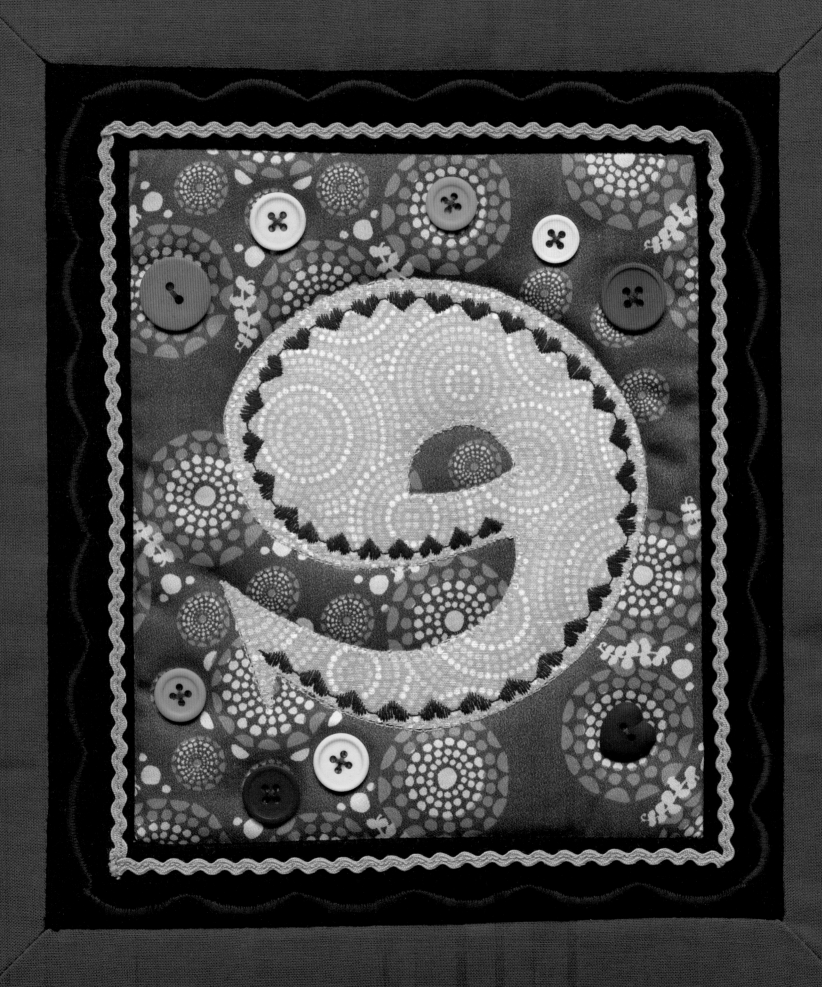

fat hen!

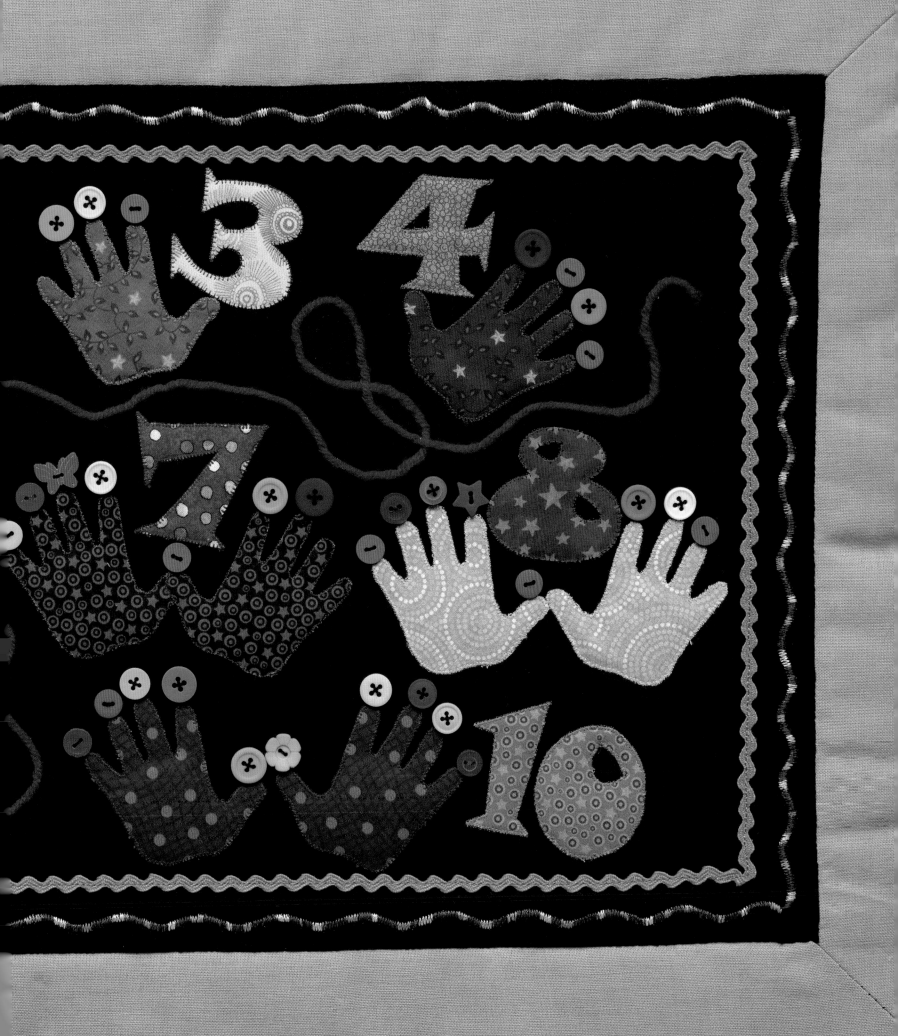

For Violet Grace

www.HarcourtBooks.com

Library of Congress Cataloging-in-Publication Data
Hines, Anna Grossnickle.
1, 2, buckle my shoe/Anna Grossnickle Hines.
p.   cm.
Summary: A child learns to count with the help of a classic nursery rhyme.
1. Nursery rhymes.   2. Children's poetry.   [1. Nursery rhymes.   2. Counting.]
I. Title.   II. Title: One, two, buckle my shoe.
PZ8.3.H556Aab   2008
[E]—dc22   2007007022
ISBN 978-0-15-206305-4

First edition
A C E G H F D B

The art for this book was
created with fabric, thread, and buttons.
The display and text type was set in Softie.
Color separations by
Bright Arts Ltd., Hong Kong
Manufactured by
South China Printing Company, Ltd., China
Production supervision by Pascha Gerlinger
Designed by Lydia D'moch